This **Walker**

book belongs to:

_____

_____

_____

For Sarah – S.McB.

For Eggert, the love of my life – L.Ó.

First published 2021 by Walker Books Ltd
87 Vauxhall Walk, London SE11 5HJ

This edition published 2022

2 4 6 8 10 9 7 5 3 1

Text © 2021 Sam McBratney
Illustrations © 2021 Linda Ólafsdóttir

The right of Sam McBratney and Linda Ólafsdóttir to be identified as author and illustrator respectively of this work
has been asserted by them in accordance with the Copyright, Designs and Patents Act 1988

This book has been typeset in Brioso Pro

Printed in China

British Library Cataloguing in Publication Data: a catalogue record for this book
is available from the British Library

ISBN 978-1-4063-9463-4

www.walker.co.uk

Mindi
and
the Goose No One
Else Could See

Sam McBratney

illustrated by

Linda Ólafsdóttir

WALKER BOOKS
AND SUBSIDIARIES
LONDON • BOSTON • SYDNEY • AUCKLAND

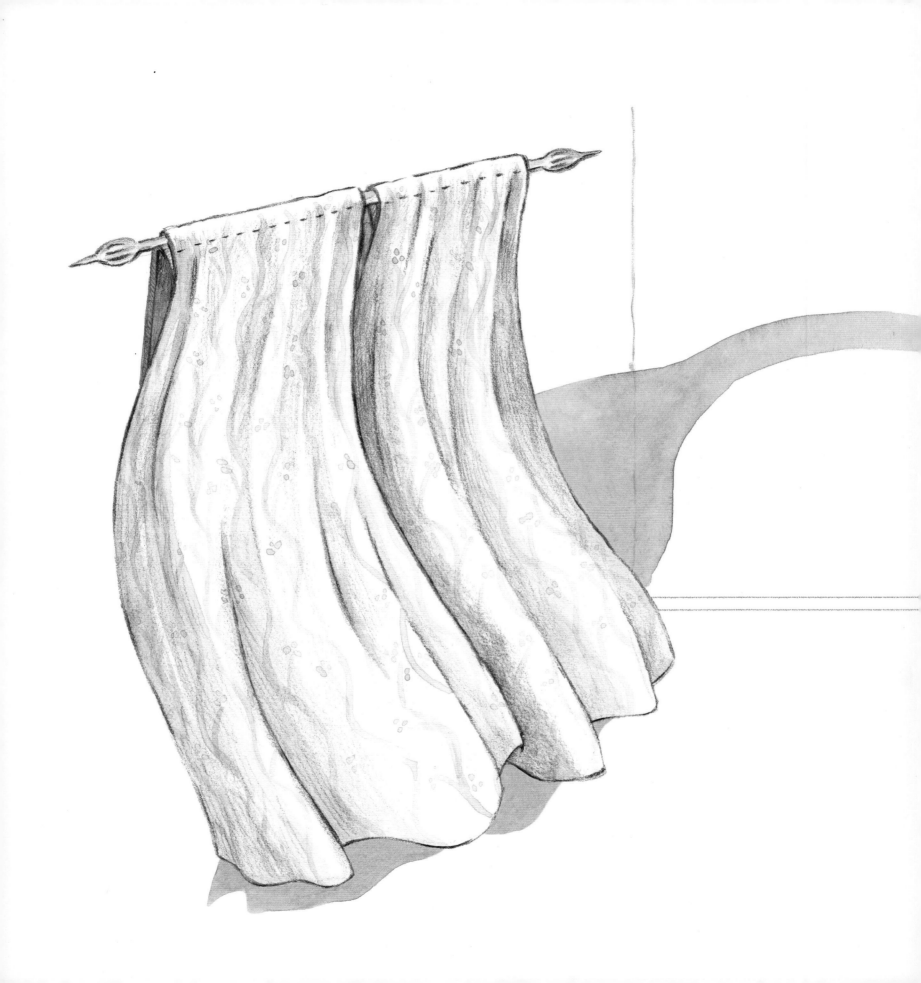

Once there was a girl called Mindi who was afraid of

something that no one else could see.

This thing that she was afraid of, this thing that

no one else could see, was a big goose.

It came into her room as quietly as a thought comes into your head,

and it stayed there for as long as it wanted to.

When she told her dad about it, he said,

"A what? There's a goose in your *room*?"

He searched high and low for the Big Goose,

but he could not find it.

Mindi's mum made fun
of it. She waved a wooden
spoon above her head,
and said, "Any goose that
comes in here will get a smack on his silly bottom!"
Mindi thought the Big Goose might be
angry about the wooden spoon.
Mum and Dad shut her window tight; but windows, walls and
doors couldn't stop the Big Goose. It came and stayed as usual.

"It isn't real, my love," her mum said.

"Nobody has a goose in their room."

"I have," said Mindi.

"Well you'll just have to close your eyes and make it *not* real!"

That night, as Mindi slept between her mummy and daddy,

her mum whispered to her dad, "We have a problem, you know.

How do we get rid of this awful goose?"

Mindi's father had been asking himself the same question.

He thought now of the wise old man called Austen, who had

helped many people in the village with sensible advice.

I'll go and see him, thought Mindi's dad.

I'll see what he has to say about geese!

Austen and his animals lived half way up

the mountain called Shelling Hill.

He greeted Mindi's dad as if he were a long-remembered friend,

and listened with care to the story of the Big Goose.

"You see what we're up against, Austen?

How can we deal with the fear of what isn't actually *there*!"

At that moment a young goat wandered over for a cuddle from Austen, who fed it an apricot. The goat swallowed the apricot, but returned the hard stone to the hand of her master.

Then Austen looked up and said, "I think you should bring your Mindi to see me. Make sure she knows I live a long way away. Make sure she knows that she is going on a *journey*."

And so it happened that Mindi and her father
set off on the journey to Shelling Hill.

When they arrived, Austen made them say hello to
the animals, including his two noisy geese;
then they went indoors for some fruit juice.

Before long, a young goat poked open the door

and wandered in as if she owned the place.

Austen passed a juicy big apricot to Mindi.

"Here. This is what she wants. Give it to her, and

if she likes you, she will give you back the stone. Let's see!"

The goat returned the stone into Mindi's small hand.

"What is her name?" Mindi asked.

"Oh, I have so many goats that I have run out of names,
I just call her Number Fifteen. What would you call her?"

"I would call her Black-and-whitey," said Mindi.

"Perfect," laughed Austen. "Black-and-whitey she shall be!"

On the way home, Mindi's dad talked

about what they had seen on Shelling Hill.

"What did you think of those two geese?" he asked carefully.

"Nice. They were nice geese." After a pause, Mindi added,

"But the BIG Goose isn't nice."

It was not the answer her father wanted to hear.

A week went by, a week of heavy rainfall
and clinging mud and sticky boots.

Mindi's mum answered a knock at the door,

and there stood Austen, dripping wet.

"Come in," she said. "Such weather to be out!"

"Sure, I never miss Market Day," said Austen,

and in he came – himself …

and a goat on the end of a rope.

Mindi recognized Black-and-whitey at once.

"Mummy, have we any apricots?"

"Dear me no, just some … plums."

"Oh, plums will do," said Austen, "goats are anything but fussy.

Now then Mindi, let's see if Black-and-whitey still likes you.

Will she give back the stone? She should, because

you gave her such a lovely name."

There was more than one plum, and therefore more than
one stone for Mindi to accept from the goat. Suddenly she threw
both arms around her and gave her a mighty neck-squasher of a hug.
Black-and-whitey seemed well pleased.

"Oh yes," smiled Austen. "You two will be friends.
I am giving her to you, Mindi!"
Little Mindi looked at the old man with an
extraordinary shine in her eyes.

Then Austen said, "But I must have something in return.
You see, it's terrible bad luck to give away an animal without
getting something back, so I thought I might exchange
Black-and-whitey for the Big Goose that no one else can see."
He paused.

It was quite a long pause.

"Would you agree to that?"

Mindi nodded once.

"The only problem is this," said Austen. "You've been to
my cottage, you know how far it is – what a journey! Along the
wide river, down the deep valleys and up those foggy hills. Foof!
You will not see that goose again."

Little Mindi seemed to be in deep thought

as she fed her goat the last of the plums.

And then she whispered to herself, as softly as could be,

"I love my Black-and-whitey."

Two quick months went by. Mindi's dad went to see the grand

old man on Shelling Hill, and said, "I came to thank you, Austen.

There has been no talk of a Big Goose since the arrival

of a certain goat – for which I must pay you."

A twinkle flickered in the red-rimmed eyes.

"Oh I'm well enough paid," the old one said. "Come and see."

Into the garden they stepped. Mindi's dad dodged the throng

of approaching goats, avoided a rooster and his ladies,

and laughed out loud as he came face to face with …

three thriving geese.

Sam McBratney, author of one of the world's bestselling picture books, *Guess How Much I Love You*, won the Bass Ireland Arts Prize and the Bisto Award, twice. He also wrote the bestselling picture-book *You're All My Favourites*.

Linda Ólafsdóttir's artwork has appeared on stamps, cereal boxes and children's clothing; she is the illustrator of a series of fairy tale retellings, published in the US, and was nominated for the Astrid Lindgren Memorial Award.